This book is dedicated to my dad, the creator of Alvin, Simon, and Theodore.
My wife and I have carried on the Chipmunk tradition since he passed away,
and we are delighted by this little book, which marries a prime-time story we wrote
in the eighties with the style he was famous for in the sixties. This book embodies
the marriage of our two Chipmunk generations, and I hope you enjoy it.

–R. B., Jr.

LITTLE SIMON
An imprint of Simon & Schuster Children's Publishing Division
1230 Avenue of the Americas, New York, New York 10020
Copyright © 2004 by Bagdasarian Productions LLC
Manufactured in the United States of America
First Edition 10 9 8 7 6 5 4 3 2 1
ISBN 0-689-87776-5

A Chipmunk Christmas

By Ross Bagdasarian and Janice Karman

Adapted by Bonnie Noelle • Illustrated by John Skewes

LITTLE SIMON

New York   London   Toronto   Sydney

In a small cottage atop the North Pole, Santa Claus was getting ready for another busy Christmas. Every Christmas and every child was special, and Santa never forgot a single one—especially those three famous singing chipmunk brothers, Alvin, Simon, and Theodore.

Alvin, Simon, and Theodore lived with David Seville. Simon was a very studious Chipmunk. Theodore was a jolly little fellow who loved to eat.

And then there was Alvin, who always had a way of getting into trouble. Sometimes it seemed Dave spent his whole day screaming . . .

"ALVIN!"

It was the first day of Christmas vacation, and the Chipmunks were extremely excited.

"Simon, Theodore, wake up! Only five more days until Christmas . . . Jingle Bells, Santa Claus, presents, and no homework!" said Alvin. "Come on, let's get Dave up."

Simon yawned and said, "I don't think Dave wants to be up this early."

But it didn't take much for the other two to convince him, and the three Chipmunks raced down the hall to Dave's room.

Alvin climbed on top of Dave's nightstand, pulled out his trusty harmonica, blew a note, and the Chipmunks did what they do best: They sang.

Dave slowly opened his eyes and sat up. "Well, good morning, boys. I see you've been practicing for today's recording session."

The Chipmunks looked at each other in shock.

"But Dave, it's Christmas vacation," said Alvin. "Couldn't we go shopping instead? For a new long board? Or a bicycle? Or a hula hoop?"

"Or encyclopedias?" asked Simon.

"Or candy?" asked Theodore.

"Or a robot? Or a spaceship? Or a stereo or TV?" rattled Alvin.

"Alvin!" shouted Dave.

"Okay!" Alvin shouted back.

It took some discussion, but Dave agreed to let the Chipmunks go shopping before the recording session. Before Dave could change his mind, the brothers were out the door and at the store.

Everyone was in the Christmas spirit. Lights decorated the windows, and wreaths hung on the walls. The store was abuzz with happy shoppers racing to make their last Christmas purchases.

Simon was busy in the toy section playing with a toy plane. Theodore was in the food department having a snack.

And Alvin? Alvin was in the music department, where he saw a little girl and her mother. They were talking about her brother, Alvin's new school friend Winchester, who was a very sick boy. His mother wanted to buy him a new harmonica, but she didn't have enough money to pay for it. Winchester's doctor bills were enormous.

Alvin couldn't believe what he had heard. He felt terrible for Winchester and his family. He wanted to help, but what could one little Chipmunk do?

Just then Simon raced over and shouted, "Come on, guys! We're late!"

Alvin, Simon, and Theodore were supposed to be at the recording studio, and Dave *hated* it when they were late.

Sure enough, the Chipmunks were late. A twenty-piece orchestra was ready and waiting for the singers in the studio. Dave became upset as he watched the musicians, who had nothing to do. Dave calculated how much money the session was costing him—even though the Chipmunks weren't there—and he wasn't happy. Luckily, the Chipmunks burst into the studio and got in position to sing just before Dave yelled, "ALVIN!!!"

"All right, fellas," Dave said with relief. "Ready to sing your song?"

"I'll say we are," replied Simon and Theodore.

"Ready, Alvin?" asked Dave.

There was no answer. Alvin was busy thinking about Winchester.

"Alvin?" Dave called out. "Alvin!" Dave cried out again, and this time Alvin heard him.

"Okay!" Alvin said, and the Chipmunks started singing.

But something was still not right. Alvin sounded flat. He couldn't concentrate on the song with Winchester and the harmonica on his mind.

The Chipmunks tried the song again, but this time Alvin sang all the wrong words.

If only there was a way to make Winchester feel better, thought Alvin. And all of a sudden Alvin knew exactly what to do. He grabbed his harmonica and ran out of the studio.

"Alvin!" shouted Dave as Alvin headed to Winchester's house.

Winchester was lying in bed, too sick to play. But boy was he happy to see Alvin.

"Merry Christmas, Winchester!" exclaimed Alvin as he handed the boy his own harmonica.

"Thank you so much!" the boy said weakly, and smiled.

It was exactly what he had wanted for Christmas. Winchester was so happy!

With a warm, fuzzy feeling in his heart, Alvin skipped back to the recording studio. He told his brothers what he had done and then sang the song perfectly from start to finish.

This time Alvin sounded fantastic.

The next day the Chipmunks and Dave decorated their Christmas tree. Simon was making a popcorn garland, and Theodore was busy eating the popcorn off the other end. Alvin was on the phone with a newspaper reporter who wanted to write a story about him and his harmonica.

Alvin handed Dave the phone and started feeling a little worried.

"It's a very special harmonica," Dave told the reporter. "I had to work three jobs to pay for it, but it was worth it. That harmonica means a lot to Alvin. In fact, he's never without it."

The Chipmunks looked at Alvin.

"What are we going to do when Dave finds out you gave your harmonica away?" asked Theodore.

"Dave will never know," said Alvin. "We just have to make some money and buy Winchester a new harmonica. Then I can get mine back."

Alvin's first moneymaking plan got off to a running start. Alvin had put on a Santa costume, and he'd gathered an odd assortment of reindeer to pull his homemade sleigh. The Chipmunks were charging one dollar per picture, and they had attracted quite a crowd.

Dave did not understand what the Chipmunks were doing. He was worried they had forgotten the true meaning of Christmas.

What are they doing now? he wondered. Dave went outside to check on the Chipmunks just as all the animals broke free from the sleigh.

"ALVIN!!!!"

After they lost the "reindeer," the Chipmunks got busy with plan number two to raise money for the harmonica. It was a beautiful day, and Alvin was sitting above a tank of water. The Chipmunks were charging money for a chance to throw a ball at the target and dunk Alvin.

Plan number three was a pre-Christmas babysitting scheme. People all over town loved this service. They were happy to have the Chipmunks watch their children so they could finish their shopping.

Dave's house was a mess, and the Chipmunks were surrounded by babies. But they had finally made some money to buy the new harmonica. Alvin just hoped it was enough.

Alvin pocketed the money and joined the rest of the shoppers at the department store. He went straight to the music section and picked up the harmonica. It was very expensive—more expensive than he had thought. Alvin didn't have enough money after all.

The sad Chipmunk didn't know what else to do, so he played a beautiful Christmas song.

After he was finished, a jolly old lady walked up to Alvin.

"That was the most wonderful thing I've ever heard," she said. "I'd like to buy that harmonica for you."

"Oh, no. I couldn't let you," Alvin replied.

"Sure you could," said the little old lady.

"Okay! Thank you!" said the grateful Chipmunk, knowing it was for a good cause.

Alvin was overjoyed. Now he could give this new harmonica to Winchester and get his own trusty one back. He was full of Christmas spirit as he played another song.

The little old lady disappeared in the crowd just as Winchester and his mother walked over to Alvin. Winchester was feeling much better. The doctor said it was a miracle. He was going to be fine.

"Having your harmonica has done so much for Winchester," his mother explained. "We read the article about you and your harmonica in the paper. It was generous of you to give it to Winchester, but we think you should have it back."

Alvin took his harmonica from Winchester and traded it for the new one. Now both boys were delighted.

Finally Christmas arrived at the Seville house, and everyone was merry.
The Chipmunks had shown Dave that they had the true spirit of Christmas all along.

Back at the North Pole, Santa and a very familiar-looking Mrs. Claus were having their own celebration. All the presents had been delivered, including an extra-special harmonica that had made a little Chipmunk and a sick little boy very happy—and that's what the spirit of Christmas is all about.